THE BOY GENIUS STRIKES AGAIN

Petie was sitting on the front porch when the Super Squad arrived. He was singing a strange song.

"What's that?" Nicole asked.

"It's called '248 Things That Start with T.' " He grinned at Annie. "I know who you are," he said.

"You do?" Annie was a little surprised since she'd never met Petie.

"Sure." Petie looked pleased with himself. "You're Annie, the missing person."

Annie looked at Nicole, who shrugged. "Who knows how he finds everything out? I think he has ESP."

THE BOY WHO REMEMBERED EVERYTHING

Jennie Abbott

Illustrated by Mary Badenhop

Troll Associates

Library of Congress Cataloging in Publication Data

Abbott, Jennie.
The boy who remembered everything.

(The Super Squad)
Summary: When a group of friends known as the Super Squad begin babysitting for a six-year-old with a fantastic memory, they find he improves all of their lives.
[1. Clubs—Fiction. 2. Baby sitters—Fiction]
I. Badenhop, Mary, ill. II. Title. III. Series.
PZ7.A156Bo 1988 [Fic] 87-14986
ISBN 0-8167-1183-6 (lib. bdg.)
ISBN 0-8167-1184-4 (pbk.)

A TROLL BOOK, published by Troll Associates, Mahwah, NJ 07430

Printed in the United States of America.
10 9 8 7 6 5 4 3 2 1

THE BOY WHO REMEMBERED EVERYTHING

Chapter 1

Marci Arnold tapped on the edge of the table and called the weekly meeting of the Super Squad to order.

"Come on, you guys," she shouted, a little louder than she intended.

Nicole, Carrie, and Annie stopped whispering and stared at her. They were all best friends and had put up with Marci's bossiness since they were kids. Annie thought Marci must have been born bossy, but Carrie didn't think so. She figured it happened when Marci's little brother, Danny, was born. Even though she was only four at the time, her parents had put her in charge of him. Added to that, Carrie figured how could the child of a chemist and a stockbroker not be bossy?

Nicole believed that Marci's bossiness began when

she started the Super Squad, or at the very least, it brought it out in her.

It started the summer after fourth grade, when they were all looking for something to do. Back then, they didn't care about money. But now, a year and a half later, they were still in the red, and there were major rumblings of dissatisfaction in Marci's basement.

"All right," Marci said. "The first order of business is the Millionaire's Fund."

Annie grinned and poked Nicole. "Some Millionaire's Fund," she said. "It's probably got ten dollars in it."

"I heard that," Marci said. She tried to look as stern as possible as she pushed her glasses over the tiny bridge of her nose. "And you're wrong. As a matter of fact, it has a hundred dollars in it."

Nicole let out a dramatic whistle and raised one fist in the air.

"A hundred dollars," she said. "We've never had that much before."

Marci picked up a computer print-out and studied it. "At this rate," she said, "we'll be millionaires by, let's see"—she squinted at the numbers—"about 2003."

"That's terrible." Annie sighed. "I'll be old and gray by then."

"You'll never be gray," Carrie assured her. "Your hair will always be that gorgeous red color." Annie smiled appreciatively at her friend.

Just as Marci was about to move on to the next order of business, Daniel, her cocker spaniel, raced down the

stairs and jumped into her lap. Daniel was named after Marci's little brother, or maybe it was the other way around—not even Marci's parents were sure anymore.

Marci petted Daniel and cleared her throat. "We have a new assignment," she said proudly. "It's a baby-sitting job."

"Oh, no," Carrie groaned. "I hope it's not like that last baby-sitting job. That kid was horrible, remember?"

"Boy, do I. The 'Terror of Tremont Street.'" Nicole sighed. "He threw stuff at me all day long—giant toy animals, pillows, spaghetti. I never wanted to see another kid again."

"What's this kid like?" Carrie asked.

"His mother says he's wonderful," Marci told her.

Everyone laughed. "Of course she told you that," Nicole grinned. "*My* mother says I'm wonderful."

"And we all know *that's* not true," Carrie teased.

Nicole tossed her long brown hair dramatically as if she were highly insulted. She was a born actress: She knew it, and so did all the other girls.

Marci picked up a Ping-Pong paddle and flipped it up into the air. "His name is Petie Franklin," she explained as she caught the paddle, "and he's six years old. His mother says he's nice, kind, brilliant, and has an amazing memory."

Everyone groaned.

"Let's face it," Carrie said, "we need the money." She looked resigned.

Annie popped out of her chair. "What about that parakeet-training assignment from . . . "

"Annie!' Everyone pounced on her. She was the smallest and youngest member of the group, so it was easy to pounce.

"We are *not* training a parakeet to dance," Marci said. Then she looked thoughtful. "At least not yet." She put the paddle down. "So for now we're stuck with Petie. And I've worked it out so Nicole gets the first day."

Nicole stood up and put her hands on her hips. "It's out of the question," she said. "My play opens in a week, and I have tons of lines to learn. Why can't someone else do it?"

"I can't because of soccer," Carrie answered.

"And I have to take Danny—my brother, that is—for his allergy shots," Marcie added. "And Annie has some mysterious family meeting tomorrow."

Annie looked away, embarrassed.

"Oh, I see." Nicole sniffed. "Everyone else has something important to do, and my play doesn't matter at all."

"Why don't you study your lines while you're baby-sitting?" Marci suggested.

Nicole looked thoughtful for a minute, then said, "I guess that's okay. I'll do it." But her heart wasn't in it.

Marci gave Petie Franklin's address to Nicole and adjourned the meeting. Then the Super Squad picked up their paddles and played three games of Ping-Pong. Carrie and Annie won all three, as usual.

"I don't get it," Nicole said to Marci as they were going up the stairs. "Why do they always win?"

Marci shrugged. "I don't know," she said. "Maybe because they look like twins."

It was a running joke among the girls. Carrie and Annie couldn't look more unalike. Where Carrie was tall, Annie was short; while Carrie had blue eyes and blond hair, Annie had green eyes and red hair.

"Oh, well," Nicole said just like she always did, "we'll get 'em next time."

The next afternoon, Nicole rushed from school and went straight to Petie Franklin's house.

Nicole started to knock on the door, but then she noticed that it was slightly ajar. She pushed it open and peeked inside. A short red-headed boy with glasses was sitting on the couch in the living room, reading a newspaper. Nicole tiptoed inside. "Hello?" she said quietly. The boy didn't look up. "Hello?" Nicole said a little louder. The boy still didn't look up.

Nicole took off her new black cape and tossed it on the couch. She unzipped her red imitation lizard boots and took them off. "Hi. I'm Nicole. I'm here to baby-sit for Petie Franklin," she said, wiggling her toes.

"Petie Franklin doesn't need a baby sitter," the boy said, without looking up.

Nicole studied the kid. He was wiry and skinny, and his hair looked like it hadn't been combed in a week. He doesn't look like any great prize to me, Nicole

thought as she remembered the "Terror of Tremont Street."

"Are you Petie?" Nicole asked.

The boy ignored the question. "So you're Nicole," he said.

Nicole nodded.

"Nicole, Nicole, I'll bet you didn't know that I can name ten Nicoles," he said after a moment.

"You can?"

"Let's see," the boy said. "There's Nicole Fouquet, the French ballet dancer, and Nicole Duplaix, the tennis player, and Nicole Martine, the writer, and—"

"Okay, okay," Nicole interrupted. "I've never heard of any of them."

"Well, none of them is very famous."

Nicole rubbed her toes and stared at the boy. "You *do* have an amazing memory." She was genuinely impressed. She hoped that Petie's mother had also been telling the truth when she said that Petie was kind and nice.

Petie stood up and put his hands in the pockets of his jeans and shrugged. "Of course I do." Then he trotted over to a table near the window. "Do you want to play chess?" he asked.

"I can't," Nicole said. "First of all, I'm a lousy chess player, because I have such a lousy memory—so you'd beat me for sure—and anyway, I have to study my lines."

Petie stood on his toes and jumped up and down.

"What lines?" he asked.

Nicole pulled her script out of her knapsack and waved it in front of Petie.

"*Now and Forever,*" she said. "It's Riverview Middle School's annual play. I play the mother, and I've got lots of lines to memorize."

"I could help you," Petie said eagerly. He looked so hopeful that Nicole almost gave in. Almost, but not quite. The idea of rehearsing with a six-year-old did not appeal to her.

"Don't you have anything else to do?" Nicole asked.

Petie shook his head.

"How about friends? Don't you have a friend to play with?"

Petie shrugged and stared at the floor. Nicole let the subject drop.

"Look," she said, "I really have to study my lines." She picked up her script. "Why don't you watch TV?" she suggested.

"It's boring." Petie sighed.

Nicole wondered if he was some kind of freak. She didn't know any kid that didn't enjoy watching television. She turned to her script as Petie picked up the newspaper and flipped to the sports section.

"Hey," he said, "do you like tennis?"

Nicole groaned. "I am *trying* to study," she said.

Petie folded the paper and put it on the floor.

"How about baseball?" he asked. Nicole ignored the question and concentrated on her script.

She began to read, "Please don't hit—

But before she had a chance to finish, Petie interrupted her again. "George Brett hit .390 in 1980," he said, and then recited the statistics of ten other baseball players who'd batted .390 during a season.

"I know," Nicole said when Petie paused to catch his breath, "we'll have to find you a friend. I can see that is the only answer to this problem."

Petie folded his arms and shrugged. "Okay," he said. "You can try, but I'm warning you, most kids don't like me very much."

"Maybe it's because you sound like a forty-year-old professor," Nicole suggested.

Petie scratched his red head and looked thoughtful. "I don't think that's it," he said after a minute.

"Then maybe it's because you're too smart," she said.

"I'm not smart," Petie stated flatly. "I've got a good memory, and I'm pretty good at chess. But that doesn't mean I'm smart."

Nicole was beginning to like the kid's directness, but she also wanted him to be quiet. The only way to get him to be quiet, she decided, was to be assertive.

"You may have a good memory," she said, "but I don't. So will you please, please, *please* be quiet?" She buried her face in her script.

Petie stared at her for a minute and tried to think of a way to distract her. Then he gave up, picked up a book, and began to read. By the end of the afternoon, Nicole had studied most of her lines, and Petie had finished two books and one newspaper.

Chapter 2

At exactly six o'clock, Petie's mother bustled through the front door. She was balancing two bags of groceries, an attache case, a pile of library books, and the evening paper. Petie rushed over, hugged her knees, and grabbed the newspaper while she put the rest of her things on the table. Then she shook Nicole's hand.

"Hi," she said breathlessly. "I'm Miranda Franklin. You must be one of the Super Squad."

"I'm Nicole."

"Well," said Mrs. Franklin, "I hope Petie wasn't any trouble."

Nicole assured her that Petie hadn't been any problem at all, although she could still hear the endless stream of facts and statistics he'd recited to her before he'd finally let her alone.

"I was studying my lines for a play I'm in," Nicole said.

Mrs. Franklin laughed. "Uh, oh," she said. "And did he let you?"

Nicole tried to give her a convincing smile. "Pretty much," she said. "I wish I had his memory. Then I wouldn't have to spend so much time studying. I could just look at the page and know my lines."

Mrs. Franklin led Nicole to the door. As she was saying good-bye, a boy of about fifteen came in. Nicole took one look at him and stepped backward. He was tall, with blond hair and large blue eyes. Mrs. Franklin introduced him to Nicole.

"This is Petie's brother, Dave," she said.

Nicole couldn't say a word. She just stared at those blue eyes and sighed. After a minute, she said good-bye to Mrs. Franklin, waved to Petie, and because Dave was so cute, of course she caught her foot and tripped as she was going out the door.

Dave took her arm to balance her, smiled, and waved at her as she went down the front walk.

She smiled back weakly, but she was so embarrassed at tripping that she wished she could disappear right then and there. She looked down at her feet and hissed, "Thanks a lot," at them.

Nicole then ran the three blocks to her house, burst through the front door, and raced up the stairs.

She threw her things onto her bed, picked up the new Princess phone that her parents had given her for her last birthday, and dialed Carrie's number. Mrs. Young told her that Carrie was still at soccer practice.

Nicole hung up the phone and dialed Annie.

"Annie," Nicole said before Annie had a chance to say hello. "It's me, Nicole. You're not going to *believe* what just happened."

"Did you baby-sit?" Annie asked in her quiet voice. Everything about Annie was little, including her voice.

Everything about Nicole was bigger than life.

"I *certainly* did," Nicole said dramatically. "The kid's okay, I guess. Well, really, he's a bit of a pain. He talks a lot, and it was hard to study my lines because he can talk and read at the same time. It's weird. And he's got this amazing memory. Computer-brain, that's a good name for him." She paused before the important part. "But that's not why I called."

"It's not?"

"No. I called to tell you about Dave."

"Who's Dave?"

"He only happens to be Petie's gorgeous older brother, that's all."

Annie's sigh traveled slowly through the telephone line.

"I know what you're thinking," Nicole said. "You're thinking that this is just another dumb Nicole crush, but you're wrong. This is *not* just another crush. This is special."

This time Annie's sigh traveled a little bit faster, but then she felt bad and apologized.

"Okay." She sighed. "Why don't you tell me about him?"

"Well," Nicole said, "he looks about fifteen. He's tall, and he's blond . . ."

When Nicole's voice trailed off dreamily, Annie tried to change the subject.

"How's the play coming?" she asked.

Nicole hesitated. "Well, okay, I guess," she mumbled. "I still have more lines to learn, but I think everything will be okay."

"I can't wait to see it," Annie said. She sounded genuinely enthusiastic.

Nicole didn't say anything. "Nicole, you *do* want us to see your play?" Annie asked.

Nicole sighed. "Sure, of course. I—I'm just a little nervous about opening night."

"Nicole," Annie said, still unconvinced. "Is something wrong?"

Nicole's voice sounded a little distant. "No, everything's fine," she said quickly. "Listen, I've got to hang up."

Annie frowned at the phone as Nicole clicked off. Something was definitely wrong, no doubt about it. But what?

Nicole, meanwhile, picked up a book, pushed her pile of stuffed animals aside, and lay down on the pink spread of her canopy bed. She tried to study, but she just couldn't concentrate.

She wondered how she was going to keep her friends away on opening night. Of course they'd expect to be there. They had seen every school play or program she'd been in since she was six. But Nicole just had to come up with some excuse to keep them away . . . .

The next morning, while Nicole was eating, the phone rang. Nicole pushed her eggs aside and answered it. It was Marci.

"Nicole?" she said brightly.

"Hmmm?"

"I know you're busy with your play and everything, but could you *please* baby-sit this afternoon?"

"For Computer-brain? No *way!*" Nicole pleaded. "I've got play practice, and I absolutely can't miss it. Why don't you call Annie or Carrie?"

"I already did," Marci said. "Carrie's got a soccer game, and Annie's not home. *Nobody's* home at Annie's as a matter of fact."

"That's funny," Nicole said. "She was there last night. I talked to her."

"Well, she isn't there now."

Nicole stretched the cord of the wall phone as far as she could and sat down at the kitchen table. She avoided her mother, who was glaring at the phone as if it were some creepy animal, and said, "Look, I can't baby-sit today. I really mean it. Please call Carrie again and see if she can get out of the game."

But Nicole knew that Carrie would never give up a soccer game. Her parents wouldn't let her. Carrie's parents took soccer and tennis and softball and ice hockey very, very seriously. If a Super Squad assignment came up at the same time as a game or a match, Carrie would definitely be at the game. No longer able to avoid her mother's glare, Nicole said, "Listen, I've got to go."

Marci called back a few minutes later. "She can't do it. She asked her parents, but—"

Nicole finished the sentence. "But they said no."

"So can you do it?" Marci asked.

"What about you?" Nicole asked. "Why can't you do it?"

"I can't. I have to take Danny to the dentist."

"Boy, if you had a dollar for every time you had to drag your little brother around, we'd already be millionaires," Nicole said.

Marci was very sensitive about being Danny's permanent baby sitter. "You think it's my favorite thing in the world? You think I like having Danny practically grafted to my hand?"

Nicole had heard this all before. "Okay, I'll try. Maybe I'll take him to play practice with me."

"That's a super idea," Marci said.

"Yeah, I guess so," Nicole said. "At least that way I can see Dave."

"Dave?"

"Petie's brother."

"Uh, oh," Marci said. "Where have I heard this before? I'm hanging up now."

"Wait, wait," Nicole cried. "What are you wearing to school today?"

Marci sighed. "The same," she said.

"Cords, flannel shirt, and blue-jean jacket?"

"Yup."

"Marci, you should experiment. You know, like I do. Why am I the only one who tries different looks?" She didn't wait for an answer. When it came to clothes, she rarely did. "Everyone always wears the same old uniform."

"That's because we're not as dramatic as you are," Marci said. "Tomorrow, I'll check out the vinyl skirts at the mall. But now I have to go."

And with that she hung up the phone.

Chapter 3

When Nicole arrived at the Franklins' house that afternoon, Petie was sitting in front of the computer, his chess set next to him.

"What are you doing?" Nicole asked.

"Trying to beat this program," Petie told her. "And I'm about to do it."

Nicole leaned over Petie's shoulder and studied the screen. "People don't beat computers, do they?" she asked.

"Sure," Petie said. "I just have a few more moves."

Nicole sat down beside him and waited. The computer made a move, and then Petie made one. No one seemed to be winning.

"Please hurry," Nicole said. "We've got to get over to my school. I have to be there for play practice."

"Just two more moves," Petie said. "And then I've got him."

Nicole waited. Petie waited. The computer waited. Nothing happened.

"Who's turn is it?" Nicole asked.

"It's his. *Shhh,* he's concentrating."

Nicole leaned back in her chair and looked toward the wall. "This is ridiculous," she said to no one in particular. "This is absolutely ridiculous. A computer doesn't concentrate. It makes a move."

"*Shhh,*" Petie said again.

Nicole waited a few more minutes, and then she tapped Petie on the shoulder.

"Your machine is down or broken or tired or something," she said. She leaned over and yanked the plug out of the wall.

Petie was furious. "Why'd ya do that?" he asked. "I was just about to win."

"Because I *have* to go to play practice," Nicole said. "And I have to go right now. Hurry up and get your jacket, and let's get out of here."

Petie put his chess set away, piece by piece.

"You are the most meticulous six-year-old I've ever seen in my whole life." Nicole sighed.

Petie grinned. "I bet you think I don't know what 'meticulous' means, but it comes from the Latin word . . . "

"I don't care where it comes from." Nicole gave him a light shove. "I just care where we're going."

Petie shrugged his shoulders and went up to his

room to find his jacket. He took a long time, and when he finally came down, Nicole was pacing up and down.

"Are you ready?" she asked, glaring at him.

Petie nodded, and he fumbled with one sleeve of his jacket as he opened the door.

"Then let's go," Nicole said, and she grabbed Petie's arm and pulled him all the way to school.

The cast of *Now and Forever* was already on the stage rehearsing when Nicole and Petie arrived. Nicole sat Petie in the back of the auditorium and ran onto the stage. It took her a few minutes to figure out what act and scene they were playing, and a few more to try and remember her line. She was still trying to remember when a voice boomed from the back of the room.

"It's the one about your daughter," Petie shouted. " 'Darling, don't stamp your foot like that or the floor might disappear.' "

Everyone on stage stared at the back of the auditorium. And for a moment, Nicole wished *she* could disappear. She could kill Petie for embarrassing her, even though she knew that he was only trying to help. Nicole certainly didn't want Mr. Lester, her director, to think that she didn't know her lines.

"Excuse me," Mr. Lester said as he peered out to the empty rows of the auditorium, "but who is that?"

"That's Computer—br—uh, I mean Petie," Nicole said nervously.

"Well, Petie seems to know your lines better than you do." Mr. Lester didn't sound angry. He sounded amused.

Nicole stared at the floor. "I guess so," she whispered. A couple of kids were giggling at her.

Then Mr. Lester sounded gentler. "Let's hope you won't be late again," he said. "And please try to remember your lines."

Nicole nodded.

The rehearsal began again. Nicole waited, practicing her next line in her mind. She wanted to hesitate a moment before saying it for effect. So when her turn came, she waited just the right amount of time, then opened her mouth to speak.

" 'I will not *stand* for this kind of behavior.' " It was Nicole's line, but not her voice. The voice was Petie's.

This time Mr. Lester didn't sound amused. "Maybe Petie should play your part," he said impatiently as he glared at the back of the auditorium.

Nicole felt like crying. She had known that line, but Petie had beaten her to it.

"Mr. Lester," Nicole said, "could I be excused for a minute?"

Mr. Lester nodded and turned to talk with one of the players. Nicole ran down the steps and walked to the back of the auditorium. She sat down beside Petie.

"Look, Major Memory," she said. "You've *got* to stop this. I mean it. I knew that line."

"I was just trying to help." Petie sulked.

"Well, don't," she snapped. "Because I don't need it."

Petie slouched down in his seat and put his knees against the seat in front of him.

"And don't look so hurt," Nicole said, feeling sorry for the kid.

When she stood up, she spotted Carrie in the back of the room. Carrie was still wearing her soccer uniform. Nicole ran over to her friend.

"Could you take it from here?" she begged. "Will you please watch him? He's driving me crazy."

"Who?" Carrie asked.

Nicole pointed to Petie.

"Meet Petie Franklin," she said. Then she thanked Carrie and ran back to the stage.

Carrie walked over and sat beside Petie. She folded her long tan legs under her and turned to look at him.

"Hi," she whispered. "I'm Carrie. I hear you're Petie."

"She's saying it all wrong," Petie said.

"What?"

Petie put his feet on the floor and sat up in his seat. "I said, she's mixing up her lines. I should help her."

Carrie put a restraining hand on his shoulder. "I don't think so," she whispered. "Maybe we should just be quiet and watch for a while."

Petie sat back in his seat and sulked some more.

"I know," Carrie said. "Let's leave. It's almost five

o'clock, and by the time we get home your mother will probably be there, right?"

"She gets home at six."

"That's okay," Carrie said. "Let's go."

Carrie and Petie slid out of the aisle and tiptoed to the back of the room. As they were about to leave the auditorium, Petie stopped and looked back at Nicole.

She was standing in the middle of the stage, poised to say a line. She took a deep breath and opened her mouth.

" 'Mr. Taggart, I presume,' " Petie shouted.

" 'Why, Mr. Taggart,' " Nicole said. " How nice to meet you.' "

One of them was obviously wrong.

Mr. Lester walked to the center stage and shaded his eyes. When he found Petie, he said, "Excuse me, Petie, but would you please refrain from helping Nicole. We have quite enough helpers, thank you."

"But she didn't know her line," Petie protested.

"I can see that," Mr. Lester said. "But that's my problem. Nicole and I will work it out together."

Petie let out a long, disgusted sigh that echoed through the auditorium.

Carrie grabbed the sleeve of his jacket and yanked him out the door. "Come on, kid," she said. "Let's go before someone murders you."

Chapter 4

Petie walked two steps behind Carrie all the way home. He refused to speak. Once or twice, Carrie tried to talk to him, but Petie wouldn't answer. Carrie figured he was kind of weird and, being a brain, was probably busy thinking.

"Did you know," he finally said as they were coming through the gate to his house, "that this town has twenty-five thousand people, and ten thousand of those people are under the age of twelve, and 4,683 of those people under the age of twelve are boys?"

"That's interesting," Carrie said absent-mindedly.

Petie brightened. "Is it? Do you really think it is? Sometimes I wonder if other people find that stuff as interesting as I do."

"Sure they do," Carrie answered. She didn't have a

12

clue whether or not anybody was interested in Petie's statistics, but her answer seemed to cheer him up.

"Aren't you the one who had a soccer game today?" Petie asked.

Before Carrie had a chance to answer, Petie said, "Did you win?"

Carrie shook her head and followed Petie through the front door. "I was terrible," she said. "Just like always. My father's going to kill me."

"Why?" Petie asked.

Carrie was beginning to understand why Nicole wanted to get rid of Petie—once the boy started talking, he had a thousand questions.

She sat down in a chair in front of the television before answering. "I missed about three shots, and of course both of my parents were there to see it. My father hates it when I blow a game."

"Everybody blows a game once in a while," Petie said, trying to reassure her. "Even Pelé, the great soccer player, blew a few. For instance, there was his first game in New York when—"

"Please," Carrie interrupted. "Give me a break. I know you're trying to be nice, but, well, you know, it doesn't really help."

"So tell me more," Petie said.

"What more?"

"Well, for instance, what do you like?"

Carrie closed her blue eyes and sighed. "Let's see," she said. "I like peppermint-stick ice cream, green sneakers, my cat, Zinger, and little boys who don't ask a million questions."

"Oh," Petie said, a bit deflated. "That's interesting."

Petie got up and went into the kitchen. He came back with two apples and handed one to Carrie. "How about some basketball?" he said. "Dave got out of his job early. He's out back shooting baskets, and maybe he'll shoot some with us."

Carrie smiled. "Sure," she agreed. "The famous Dave. By all means, let's play."

Carrie and Petie went through the back door to the driveway. Dave was concentrating so hard on dribbling the basketball that he didn't notice them.

"Watch this," Carrie whispered to Petie as she sneaked up behind Dave and bounced the ball away from him. She dribbled the ball down the driveway and turned to throw a long shot. The ball swished the basket without touching the rim.

"Wow," David said. "That was awesome."

Carrie shrugged and kicked a stone across the driveway.

"I guess you're Dave," she said. "I'm Carrie, a Super Squad baby sitter."

Carrie could tell that Dave wasn't listening. "That was some basket," he said again. "Maybe we could have a pickup game."

"That sounds good to me," Petie said.

Dave glanced at Carrie and shrugged. "I didn't exactly mean you, kid," he said.

Petie looked so sad that Carrie felt sorry for him. "Oh, come on," she said. "He'll be okay. Let's let him play."

Dave bounced the ball four times and then said, "All right. But the kid's so small that he may get hurt. Tell you what. Let's just shoot some baskets and see who can sink the most."

Petie stamped his foot. "I am *not* small," he declared. "And I'm a much better basketball player than you are."

Dave laughed. "Oh, yeah," he said. "We'll see about that."

Petie lined up behind Dave and Carrie and waited his turn. Dave handed the basketball to Carrie and said, "Okay, superstar, you're first. Let's see what you can do."

Carrie took a few steps to the left and poised the ball above her head. She let it go, and the ball whizzed through the basket.

Carrie retrieved the ball and tossed it to Dave. Dave stood where Carrie had stood a few minutes before and tossed the ball. It missed the basket by inches and ricocheted off the backboard.

Petie ran up, retrieved the ball, then tossed a jump shot. The shot missed.

Carrie could tell that Dave was annoyed. "Let's try again," he said.

The three of them shot baskets for the next hour. When Mrs. Franklin arrived, the score was Carrie 10,

Petie 4, and Dave 2. Dave insisted that he was having a bad day, but Petie swore that it was a day just like any other.

"Dave's just a lousy basketball player," Petie said, planting his hands firmly in his pockets.

Dave grinned. "You know, he's right," he said to Carrie. "Maybe you could help me."

"I guess I could manage a few lessons," she said.

"Tomorrow?" Dave asked.

"I have soccer practice tomorrow," Carrie told him. "Wait a minute. Oh, no. It's also my turn to baby-sit."

"For me?" Petie asked.

Carrie pushed Petie's red hair out of his eyes. "Who else?" she asked gently.

"No problem," Petie said. "I'll just go to soccer practice with you. I'll sit on the bench and be real, real quiet. I promise."

Everyone laughed. Petie had never been quiet in his whole life.

Dave and Petie walked Carrie to the gate. Dave punched her gently on the arm and said good-bye.

"See you tomorrow," Carrie said.

"Right," Dave said. "Say, I have an idea. Why don't I drop Petie off at soccer practice. I can't stay long, but at least I can see you in action." Carrie agreed and said good-bye.

As she was walking home, she ran into Marci and Danny. Marci was carrying a small paper bag with the words INSIDE OUT—THE CRAZIEST BOUTIQUE IN TOWN written on it. "What is *that*?" Carrie asked, pointing to the bag.

Marci laughed and opened the bag. "Something gaudy. Nicole says I'm too conservative and that I should experiment with my clothes more."

"She says we're all too conservative." Carrie chuckled.

"So I bought something very, very gaudy."

Marci held up a pink-and-blue-sequined bracelet.

Carrie frowned. "It's gaudy, all right," Carrie agreed. "Before you know it, you'll be wearing capes and tiaras like Nicole."

Marci laughed and waved. "Don't count on it," she said as she put the bracelet back in the bag and headed home.

I'll bet she never wears that thing, Carrie thought as she turned the corner.

Carrie's parents were sitting in the living room when she walked in the door.

"There you are," her father said. "Would you come in for a few minutes? I want to talk to you."

Carrie went into the living room and sat on the couch.

"It's about the game, right?" She sighed and began to twirl her hair nervously around her fingers.

"I know you're trying," her father said. "But something's wrong."

Carrie shrugged. She didn't want to talk about the

game. All she wanted to do was go upstairs and call Annie. Carrie had heard all of this before.

"I didn't mean to miss the shots, Dad," she said.

"I know you didn't. But what happened?"

I'm a lousy soccer player, Carrie thought, and a lousy athlete. But she didn't say anything. She just shrugged.

"You're too good to be playing like this," Mr. Young said harshly.

Carrie shrugged again.

Her father sighed.

After a few minutes of silence, Carrie asked, "Are we finished for now?"

"I guess so," her father said.

Carrie bolted out of the room and ran upstairs. She rushed into her room and started to straighten it. She rearranged her swimming and tennis trophies and put her six pairs of sneakers in order. Carrie always straightened things when she was upset. It was her way of adding order to her life. When she was finished, she called Annie. No one answered, so she dialed Nicole's number. Nicole answered after the second ring.

"It's me, Carrie."

"I heard about the game," Nicole said. "Sorry."

"Yeah, well, thanks. But that's not what I'm calling about. Have you heard from Annie? She wasn't in school today and no one answers the phone. Where do you think she is?"

"I don't know. It's weird." She paused. "I talked

to Annie last night, and she didn't say she was going anywhere."

"Well, I'm worried," Carrie said. "If she didn't come to school because she's sick, then she should be home, right?"

"Unless she's ver-r-r-y sick," Nicole pointed out.

Carrie thought that Nicole was being a little dramatic, but Annie *was* missing, after all.

"By the way," Nicole said as casually as she could manage, "did you meet Dave?"

"Oh, sure," Carrie said. She didn't sound very excited to Nicole.

"He's cute, don't you think?"

"He's okay, I guess. But," she added, "he's a lousy basketball player."

"You played *basketball* with him?" Nicole cried. She would have given anything to have gotten that close to Dave.

"Sure, but it was no big deal," Carrie said. "I told you he wasn't a major talent."

Nicole was strangely silent. Then she said a quick good-bye and hung up the phone.

Chapter 5

Carrie was kicking balls into the goal when she heard a high-pitched whistle. It was Petie, of course, along with Dave. Carrie waved, then ran over to the sidelines to say hello.

"We were watching you," Dave said.

"You were?"

"Yup. For about fifteen minutes. I made Petie promise to be quiet for once in his life, and guess what, he managed it."

"I'm quiet a lot," Petie said.

Carrie laughed. "Well," she said, "what do you think?"

"You're good," Dave said, and Carrie could tell that he meant it. Carrie muttered a thank-you and dug the toe of her shoe into the ground.

"Come on, Carrie, let's go," one of her teammates called.

Carrie waved and ran back to practice. She kicked the ball across the field to another player, and when it came back to her, she kicked it into the net. As she walked back to center field, she noticed her father sitting on a bench near Petie and Dave. Her heart sank a little at the sight of her father, but she waved, and Dave waved back.

Oh, no, he thought I was waving to him, Carrie thought.

As Carrie watched, Dave cuffed Petie on the head and walked away. Petie went over to the bench and sat beside Carrie's father.

After Dave left, things went from bad to worse. Nothing seemed to go right for Carrie. She missed every shot on goal, and most of the other shots that came her way.

When practice was over, she slowly walked over to the bench, sat down next to her father, and took a deep breath.

"Hi," he said. Carrie could tell by the tone of his voice that he wasn't pleased.

"Dad, this is Petie," Carrie said. Petie held out his hand, and Carrie's father shook it.

"She's baby-sitting for me," Petie said. He took his glasses off and wiped them on his jacket. "Don't worry, Mr. Young," Petie continued. "I think I know what's the matter. All she needs is a little coaching, and a few Franklin statistics. The first shot was just a

few inches off, the second bounced off the pole, the third—"

"Okay, Petie," Carrie cut him off. "Dad doesn't care about that."

"No, go on," Carrie's father disagreed. "I *do* care. Go on, young man." He stared at Petie in amazement.

Petie went on to document every move, every shot. When he was finished, Carrie's father was impressed.

"Well, with all that information at your fingertips, you should be able to improve quite a bit, don't you think so, Carrie?"

Carrie was thinking that she didn't want to improve. All she wanted to do was quit the team.

But Carrie didn't say that. "I'll see you later, Dad. I have to take Petie home." Then she grabbed Petie's arm and started walking.

"Try kicking it a little more to the left when you're standing on the right side," Petie told her.

Carrie didn't say anything.

"And you moved a little too fast on the fourth pass. Slow down a little."

Carrie was beginning to hate Petie.

"Look," she said, "I don't even want to play soccer. I'm terrible at it."

"Then why don't you quit?"

"Because I can't. Because my father would kill me. Because I don't know how to quit. I don't know." She sighed. "And why am I telling my problems to a six-year-old?"

"Boy." Petie sighed. "All I was trying to do was help."

Dave was waiting in the driveway. He tossed the ball to Carrie. "You're up," he said. Carrie tossed the ball through the basket. Dave retrieved it and tossed it back to her. "Again," he said. Carrie took a jump shot.

"Bull's-eye," Dave said.

Carrie made four baskets in a row, but they didn't help her spirits at all.

"What's the matter?" Dave asked.

"She wants to quit the soccer team," Petie told him. "And she doesn't know what to do."

"Why don't you just quit?" Dave asked.

Carrie shrugged.

"Her father won't let her," Petie said.

"Can't she speak?" Dave asked.

Carrie looked at Petie and Dave discussing her life. Suddenly the whole situation seemed funny, and Carrie began to laugh. She laughed and laughed until she couldn't laugh anymore. "I'll figure it out," she said when she'd caught her breath. "But thanks, Petie, for your concern."

After a while Petie went inside to watch television, and Dave and Carrie sat down on the grass.

"Are you sure you want to quit?" Dave asked.

"Not completely sure. I've tried, but I'm just a lousy soccer player."

Dave smiled. "Well," he said, "I guess we're all

lousy at something. I don't happen to be so great at basketball, in case you haven't noticed."

Carrie laughed. "You're not so bad," she said. Carrie stood up and brushed herself off. "Well, I guess I should get home."

"What about the team?" Dave asked. "Are you going to quit?"

"I don't know. I'll think about it."

She went inside to say good-bye to Petie. He trotted beside her to the front door.

"Don't forget," he said. "If you decide not to quit, just call, and I'll go over those plays that need improvement."

"I won't forget," Carric said, and playfully tapped Petie on the head.

When Carrie got home, she went straight to the phonc. She called Annie again, but no one answered. Then she called Marci.

"Have you seen Annie?" Carrie asked when Marci answered.

"No, have you?"

"I'm getting worried," she said.

"Maybe we should go over to her house," Marci suggested. "There might be something wrong."

They agreed to meet in an hour; then Carrie went downstairs for dinner.

No one mentioned the game or soccer practice or Carrie's lack of enthusiasm for the sport. She hadn't made up her mind about quitting yet.

Carrie was finishing her dessert when the doorbell rang. She got up from the table and answered it.

Marci was dressed in her usual conservative outfit, with one exception. She was wearing the pink-and-blue-sequined bracelet. Carrie smiled when she saw it. "It's Marci," Carrie called to her parents. "We're going over to Annie's to see if she's all right."

"What's wrong?" her father asked.

"I don't know, but she hasn't been at school, and no one answers her phone. We're sort of worried about her."

"Well, be back early," her mother said.

Carrie and Marci ran to Annie's house and rang the doorbell. When no one answered, Carrie stepped back and looked up at the windows.

"No lights," she said. "It looks like no one's home."

"Hmmm," Marci said. "This is very strange."

Chapter 6

"By the way," Marci said as she and Carrie walked home from Annie's, "I've invested the Squad's money in a new computer stock."

"I'll bet that's risky business," Carrie said.

"Not really. The way I see it, we should double our money within the next month. I figured it all out. If I can double the money every month, we'll be millionaires before you know it."

Carrie grimaced. "Definitely risky," she said. "This is the last time," she added, "that I'm going to work for nothing."

Marci looked sympathetic. "Well, you've put in more than your share on this job, and I want you to know I really appreciate it. With Annie missing, Nicole's play, and my little brother—well, anyway, thanks."

"It's okay," Carrie said. "I'll be there tomorrow."

"No, don't," Marci said. "Tomorrow's Nicole's turn. Well, really, it's mine, but Nicole has volunteered to take my place, and I did want to follow up on that computer stock."

"Sounds like Nicole really wants to baby-sit," Carrie said.

Marci glanced over at her friend, but it was too dark to see the look on her face.

"She calls every day, begging to sit. She's got a crush on Dave, so she wants to spend some time there."

"Oh," Carrie said. All of a sudden she felt a little strange. "What about play practice?"

"That's another thing. Every time I mention the play, Nicole acts real weird. I don't think she wants any of us to come to the play, and I can't figure out why."

"She's been having trouble with her lines," Carrie said. "So maybe she's afraid she'll blow it."

Marci thought for a minute, and then she said, "No, I don't think that's it. We've seen her blow her lines plenty of times before. It must be something else."

"Well, maybe I'll stop by at play practice tomorrow and see what's up," Carrie said.

When they got to Marci's house, Carrie waved good-bye and ran up the sidewalk. When she got to the corner, she turned and looked back. All she could see were the pink-and-blue sequins glittering in the dark.

*　　*　　*

The next afternoon, Carrie skipped soccer practice and went into the auditorium to check out play rehearsal.

Petie was sitting in the back row, reading a book. Carrie went over and sat beside him. She folded her legs under her and tapped him on the shoulder.

"Hey," Petie said. "What're you doing here?"

"*Shhh.* I just thought I'd watch the play."

Petie sat up straighter in his chair and turned to stare at her. "I don't get it," he said. "You're supposed to be at soccer. This is Nicole's day."

"Look, Petie, will you *please* keep your voice down?"

"Well, Nicole isn't going to like this," Petie said in a louder whisper. "She's dying to walk me home after play practice." He rolled his eyes at the ceiling for emphasis.

"Because of Dave?"

Petie nodded. Carrie and Petie sat back in their chairs and watched the play. After a while Carrie said, "Petie, do you have any idea why Nicole doesn't want us to see the play? She doesn't seem so bad to me."

"She isn't. That's not the problem."

Carrie glanced at Petie. "What *is* the problem?" she asked.

"I promised not to tell." Petie smiled mysteriously.

Carrie poked him. "Come on," she said. "You can tell me."

Petie shook his head violently. "I promised, I

promised, I promised. Did George Washington break his promises? Did Abe Lincoln break his promises? Would you break a promise?''

Carrie slumped back in her seat and folded her arms. ''Oh, forget it,'' she mumbled.

When play practice was over, Nicole ran down from the stage and joined them. She didn't seem very happy to see Carrie.

''I thought you had soccer,'' she said.

''I didn't go.''

Nicole wasn't surprised. ''Oh, I see,'' she said sarcastically. ''Can't decide if you want to quit the team or not, huh? Well, I guess you'll decide before school is out.'' Nicole grabbed Petie's arm and pulled him toward the door.

''Wait a minute,'' Petie said. ''Carrie's coming with us.''

''She *is*? Why?''

''Dave asked me to give him some basketball lessons,'' Carrie told her. The minute she finished her sentence, she knew that she had said the wrong thing.

Nicole glared at her.

''Look, Nicole,'' Carrie said, ''we're just going to shoot a few baskets, that's all. You can shoot some, too.''

Nicole stopped at her locker and took out some books. ''I'm terrible at basketball,'' she said as she slammed the door shut.

Petie laughed. "That's okay," he said. "So's Dave. You can be terrible together."

It was obvious that Petie was getting a great deal of pleasure out of this little drama.

"Oh, all right," Nicole agreed. "I'll try it."

Carrie was silent as she walked to Petie's. She kept thinking about the play and Nicole's hesitation about their coming to it. When they were almost to Petie's, Carrie decided to mention it.

"Nicole," she said carefully, "why don't you want us at your play?"

"I didn't say that," Nicole said, walking a little faster.

Carrie hurried to keep up with her. "But you act like you don't want us there," she said.

Nicole stopped and looked at Carrie. "I don't," she said. "But I'm just being silly, and well, really, I don't want to talk about it anymore. Okay?"

Carrie nodded, but she wasn't satisfied. Something was definitely wrong.

Dave was shooting baskets when they arrived. He cradled the ball under his arm and walked up to Carrie. "Are you ready?" he asked. "I've been practicing all afternoon."

"Nicole's going to play, too," Carrie said.

Dave glanced at Nicole and smiled. "Sure," he said. "And what about Petie?"

"I'm not playing," Petie said. "I'm just going to sit and watch. This should be very interesting." He plunked

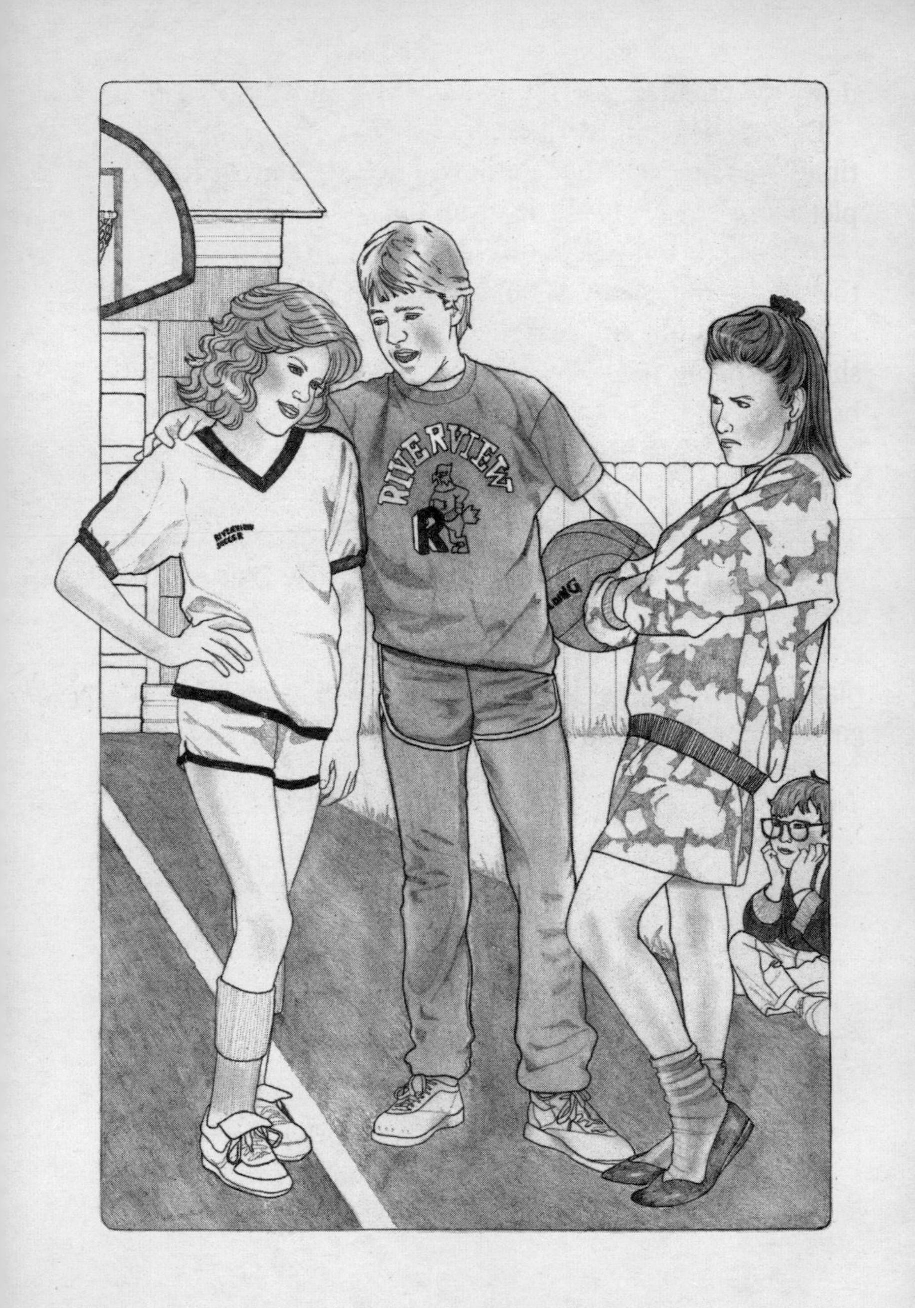
RIVERVIEW
R

down on the lawn and cupped his chin in his hand.

Dave threw the ball to Nicole. She dribbled it three times and shot it. The ball missed the backboard completely.

"Don't worry," Dave said as he ran up and retrieved the ball. "There's always another shot."

He tossed the ball to Carrie, and Carrie took a long shot, hitting the basket perfectly. Dave patted her on the back.

"Great shot. Don't you ever miss?" he asked.

Nicole held out her arms for the ball. "Let me try again," she said nervously.

Dave threw her the ball, and she tossed it toward the basket. The ball missed the backboard again. Nicole cringed inside. She was humiliating herself in public. The play was one thing, but this was worse. She quickly gathered her things and walked toward the house.

"I'd better go," Carrie whispered to Dave as she watched Nicole leave. "I'll see you tomorrow, okay?"

Dave nodded.

Carrie ran after Nicole. When she caught up to her, she said, "Look, Nicole, I know how you feel."

"No, you don't."

"Sure I do. I've been jealous before."

Nicole spun around and glared at Carrie. "I am *not* jealous. I am *not* upset. I am *not* anything. I am merely going home."

And then she shook her hair and ran down the sidewalk.

Chapter 7

The phone was ringing as Carrie walked in the front door. She ran into the kitchen and picked it up.

"It's me," Marci said. "Could you come over after dinner?"

"Did you hear something about Annie?" Carrie asked.

"No," she said softly. "It's just that I want to talk with you and Nicole. I have to make a decision tonight."

"Sounds pretty serious."

"It is."

"I'll be there if I can get past my father," Carrie said. "There's another game tomorrow, and you know how he is about 'staying in training.' " She dropped her voice to imitate her father.

"Well, try. I'm going to call Nicole now, and I'll tell her seven-thirty, okay?"

"I guess," Carrie said hesitantly.

Carrie hung up the phone and went into the dining room. Her father was sitting at the table paying bills.

"Can I eat early?" Carrie asked. "I have to go over to Marci's."

Mr. Young looked up and smiled. "Big game tomorrow," he reminded her.

Carrie sat down at the table and pushed a pile of checks aside. "Dad," she said, "could I talk to you?"

"Sure," her father said, pushing back his chair.

Carrie picked up a pencil and twirled it. She felt as if her tongue couldn't move. "I don't think I want to play soccer anymore," she said.

Mr. Young sat back in his chair and stared at Carrie over his glasses. "Why not?" he asked. Carrie could tell that he hadn't expected this.

"Because I'm a lousy player," she said. "And I don't really like it."

Mr. Young shrugged and went back to his bills. "It's up to you," he said. "I guess if you want to quit, well, then . . ."

"It's not quitting, Dad. Really. I just don't like it."

Mr. Young wrote another check. "Whatever you decide, Carrie," he said.

Carrie waited a while. But when her father didn't say anything else, she stood up and went to her room. She straightened her trophies, and then she lay down on her bed.

Mr. Young didn't mention the game again until Carrie was leaving for Marci's.

"I'm sure you'll make the right decision," he said. And when Carrie didn't answer, he said, "Good night."

"Good night, Dad," Carrie said, being careful not to slam the door behind her. The last thing she needed was to have her father think she was angry at him, even if she was.

Marci's mother let Carrie in and pointed in the direction of loud music coming from the basement. Marci and Nicole were sitting on the floor, listening to a tape that was so loud they didn't look up until Carrie shouted for the third time.

Marci jumped up. "You made it," she cried. "What about the game?"

"My Dad's giving me a hard time about it," she said. "But here I am."

"Here you are," Nicole said sarcastically. Nicole was dressed in her preppy look. She was wearing corduroy pants, a down vest, and Topsiders. Nicole always dressed preppy for a late-night Squad meeting.

"Hi, Nicole," Carrie said, trying to be friendly. But Nicole obviously wasn't ready to forgive and forget.

"Could we just get on with the meeting," she said, "so I can get home and do my homework?"

Carrie figured she must be really annoyed. After all, who would want to rush anywhere to do homework?

Marci picked up a computer print-out and said, "I've called this meeting because I have to decide what to do about that computer stock."

Nicole groaned. "Oh, no, we're broke again," she said.

"Is that right?" Carrie asked Marci. Carrie was trying to sound nice, but she was beginning to feel annoyed. First her father, now this.

Marci nodded. "Yes," she said softly. Then she brightened a bit. "But if we sell the stock right now, maybe we can still keep a little money."

"Like how much?" Carrie asked. Her voice had a tense edge to it.

Marci studied the print-out carefully. After a while she looked up and said apologetically, "Well, maybe about twenty dollars. Or a little less."

Nicole groaned again. "Why am I working for this outfit?" she asked of no one in particular. "Why don't I just go be a volunteer somewhere? Then at least I wouldn't have to put up with kids like Petie who have impolite, insensitive, older brothers."

"I thought you were working toward a new stereo," Marci said.

"It's turning out to be more like a new stereo needle," Nicole pointed out.

Carrie was starting to feel sorry for Marci. "I say we don't sell it now," she said. "You never know. It might go back up, and then, well, who knows? Twenty dollars isn't much. Let's gamble."

"Nicole?" Marci said.

Nicole shrugged. "I don't care," she said. "I guess Carrie's right. One fourth of twenty is five, and I can't buy a stereo for five dollars. I can't even buy a needle. So okay, I say keep it."

Carrie stood up and flipped the tape. "It's not one fourth these days," she said as the music began to blare. "It's one third. Where *is* Annie anyway? I'm getting very worried."

"No one knows," Nicole said.

"Well," Carrie said, "tomorrow I'm going to the principal and find out. I can't stand it any longer."

Nicole and Marci agreed that that sounded like a good idea. "Mr. Freid must know where she is. Principals know everything," Marci said.

Carrie went over to turn down the music, and Marci walked over to Nicole.

"How's the play?" she asked.

"It's okay," Nicole said.

"I can't wait to see it," Carrie said. "Saturday night, isn't it?"

Nicole nodded and grabbed her vest from the back of the chair. "Look, Carrie," she said as she put it on. "I really wish you wouldn't come."

"Because of Dave?"

"No," Nicole said emphatically. "Not because of Dave. I don't care anything about Dave." She didn't sound very convincing. "I just don't want my friends there. So please don't come." And with that she raced up the stairs and slammed the front door.

"What is going on?" Carrie asked when Nicole was gone.

"I don't know," Marci answered. "But there sure is a lot of weirdness going around. Annie's missing. Nicole's being Miss Secretive about this play. And, worst of all, my stock is falling by the minute."

"Not to mention my game," Carrie added as she followed Marci upstairs.

Marci stopped at the top of the stairs and turned around. "Tomorrow's game?" she asked.

"Yup. I'm thinking of quitting the team."

Marci stared down at Carrie, perplexed. "You *can't* quit the team," she said. "You're one of the best players on it."

Carrie couldn't believe her ears. She wasn't one of the best players at all. "I'm terrible," she said.

"You are *not*. I'll bet if you look at the statistics, you'll see that you're right up there on top." Marci shook her head. "I can't believe you're saying this."

"Well, *I* think I'm terrible." She was staring at her fingernails.

Marci waited while Carrie went through the basement door, then closed it.

"You always think you're terrible," she said.

"My *father* thinks I'm terrible," Carrie reminded her.

Marci chuckled. "That, dear Carrie, is your problem," she said. "Believe me, you are not terrible, and I think you should play tomorrow. Besides, it's my day to baby-sit for the incredible Petie, and I need someplace to take him."

Carrie opened the front door. "Well," she said, "I'll think about it tonight."

As Carrie walked down the walk, Marci called after her. "Don't forget. You're going to ask Mr. Freid about Annie tomorrow, okay?"

"How can I forget that?" Carrie asked.

Chapter 8

The next morning, Carrie got to school ten minutes early and went straight to Mr. Freid's office. The door was open, and when Mr. Freid saw her, he motioned for her to come in and sit down.

Carrie ignored the chair beside his desk and stood in front of him. She could feel her hands becoming damp, just like they always did when she went into Mr. Freid's office.

"I was wondering if you know anything about Annie," Carrie said.

"Annie?" Mr. Freid asked.

"Annie Lewis. She hasn't been in school for days, and we've been trying to call her, and no one answers, and—"

"Whoa," Mr. Freid said. "As a matter of fact, I do

know about Annie. She's okay, and she'll be in school on Monday, but I think she'll be home tomorrow."

"She will?"

Mr. Freid nodded and picked up a pencil. "And as for your next question," he said, "I'm afraid that I can't say where she's been. She'll have to tell you that herself."

Carrie thanked him and went to her first class. Marci was sitting in her regular seat by the window.

"Well," she whispered when Carrie sat down beside her, "what did he say?"

"He said that she'll be home tomorrow and in school on Monday. But the whole thing is very mysterious. He won't tell me where she's been."

"Probably on a modeling assignment." Marci chuckled to herself, obviously pleased with her little joke.

"Very funny," Carrie said. "Can you imagine Annie on a modeling assignment? She hates having her picture taken for the yearbook."

"They always like redheads though," she said.

"Be serious," Carrie said. "I wonder what happened to her."

"I guess we'll have to wait until tomorrow," Marci said.

Now that she knew Annie was all right, Carrie's thoughts returned to her main worry, her upcoming soccer game. She still didn't know if she was going to play, and every time she thought about it, she felt a little sick.

After last period, Carrie gathered up her books and headed toward the locker room. She was halfway down the stairs when she changed her mind and started back up. Marci was coming down, and Carrie bumped right into her.

"Watch it, kid," Marci laughed.

Carrie looked up, and when she saw Marci, she looked surprised.

"Aren't you supposed to be on your way to the game?" Marci asked.

"I guess so," Carrie said as she tried to brush past Marci.

Marci grabbed Carrie's arm. "Wait a minute, Carrie," Marci said. "What are you doing?"

Carrie shook herself free and ran up the stairs. She ran into the library and sat at a table in the back. She looked around to make sure that no one she knew was there, and then she opened a book and pretended to study.

A few minutes later, Petie came in. Carrie noticed him out of the corner of her eye, and she slumped down in her seat so that he wouldn't see her. But Petie spotted her right away. He ran over and tapped her on the shoulder.

"What are you doing *here*?" he shouted.

"*Shhh,*" Carrie said. She looked around nervously. "Don't you know you're in a library?"

"What are you doing *here*?" Petie whispered.

Carrie held up her science book and showed it to

Petie. "I'm studying. Can't you see that?" Carrie said too loudly.

"*Shhh,*" Petie said, looking around. When he was satisfied that they hadn't bothered anyone, he added, "But why aren't you at the game? Your coach is looking all over for you. He's very upset."

Carrie sighed. She just wished Petie would go away. "First of all," she said, "what are you doing here?"

"Dave brought me, and Marci said she saw you heading this way. Marci sure was glad she didn't have to watch me."

Carrie looked up, surprised. "Dave brought you?"

"Yup, and he's wondering where you are, too."

"Well," Carrie said, "I'm not playing. I can't. I've decided to quit the team."

"Your parents are there, too," Petie said.

Carrie groaned.

Petie sat back in his chair and tipped it back on its hind legs. "I think you should play," he said. "I'll help you. You have the talent; you just need a few pointers. I think I know every play you ever made. I know the ones that work and the ones that don't. I'll just tell you what to do, and you'll do fine." He sounded completely sure of himself.

Carrie couldn't help but smile. "Thanks, Professor," she said. Even Petie had to laugh at that.

"Does my father look angry?" Carrie asked.

Petie screwed up his mouth a bit. "No. He mostly looks like he's thinking about something."

Carrie gathered up her books and stood up.

Petie jumped up so fast he almost knocked his chair over. "Are we playing?" he asked.

Carrie shrugged and laughed. "I guess we are," she said.

Petie smiled a big smile and whistled his high-pitched whistle. Everyone in the library looked up.

"Oh, great," Carrie whispered. "Now I won't be able to show my face around here either."

Petie laughed as he followed Carrie down to the locker room. He waited outside while she changed into her uniform, and then he followed her down to the field. As she walked to the bench, Carrie could feel her father's eyes following her. She knew that Dave was watching her, too.

"Well, Carrie," her coach said as she walked up. "I see you decided to join us."

Carrie couldn't tell if he was angry or not, so she didn't answer. She just shrugged and smiled.

"Well," he said more gently, "we're glad you did, because we're going to need you today. Get out there."

Carrie turned and bumped smack into Petie. "Are we ready?" he asked hopefully.

"I guess so," Carrie said.

Petie shot her a victory sign. "Okay, then, here we go. First of all, don't and I mean *don't* do what you did in practice."

Carrie started walking toward the field. Petie walked double-step beside her.

"It was in the second period. Number fourteen kicked the ball to you, and you stepped backward. That threw you off just enough to miss your shot on goal. This time just stand still and wait."

Carrie nodded and raced out to the field. She took her place and waited for the referee to blow the whistle. A few minutes later, number fourteen kicked her the ball. She stood perfectly still and waited. Then she kicked it hard, and the ball slammed into the goal. The crowd cheered.

Carrie jumped up into the air, hugged her teammates, then ran over and hugged Petie.

"Want to do it again?" he asked.

Carrie nodded.

"Number twelve on the other team."

"What about her?"

"She's always three paces behind. She just doesn't get started on time. Be sure to pass the ball in front of her."

Carrie listened intently. Then she smiled at Petie. "Gotcha," she said. As she ran back to her position, she passed Petie's information on to the rest of the team.

The team passed the ball in front of number twelve whenever they had a chance, and on the third pass, Carrie ran a bit ahead of her, caught the pass, and scored another goal. The spectators roared their approval.

Carrie looked over at Petie and raised her fist in the air.

Petie was sitting on the bench between Dave and Carrie's father. Carrie could tell by the looks on their faces they were all very pleased with her.

As she was taking her position again, she noticed that Nicole was sitting on the other side of Dave. She must have gotten out of play practice early. She was wearing her free-and-easy look—sweater, a long blue skirt, her hair pulled up in a casual ponytail. She stared at the ground when Carrie looked at her. Carrie knew she was miserable because of Dave, but she had no idea what to do about it.

Carrie pushed everything out of her mind but the game. Between periods, Petie provided vital statistics, and in the second period Carrie scored two more goals. By the end of the game, the score was 6-2 in favor of Riverview, and Carrie had scored four of the goals.

Carrie ran off the field, grabbed a towel, and sat down on the bench between her father and Petie.

"Congratulations," her father said. "You're quite a star." He gave her a big hug.

Carrie sat on her hands and dug her toe into the dirt.

"No, I mean it," her father said. "I'm glad you decided not to quit."

"So am I," Carrie said. "But most of the credit has to go to Petie."

"Aw, shoot," Petie said, looking falsely modest.

Carrie punched him. "Don't get humble on me," she said. "Really, you saved the day."

"Aw, shoot," Petie said again, and everyone laughed.

They were still laughing when Dave came over to congratulate her. He shook her hand and patted her on the shoulder.

"You're a better soccer player than you are a basketball player," he said. "And that's saying a lot."

Carrie thanked him and looked over to the next bench where Nicole was now sitting. She looked forlorn as she watched Carrie and Dave. Carrie smiled at her, but Nicole didn't smile back. Instead, she stood up and walked toward the school. Carrie felt terrible. She ran her hands through her blond hair and tried to think of what to do about Nicole.

Chapter 9

Carrie thought about Nicole all evening. She tried to call her twice, but she couldn't dial the phone. She didn't know what to say.

At nine o'clock she called Marci instead.

"Look, Marci," she said. "I'm really upset about Nicole. She's mad at me about Dave, and I don't know what to do about it."

"Forget it," Marci said. "Nicole's just upset that Dave likes you better than he likes her. Don't worry, she'll find a new crush in a few days."

"But I hate not having someone like me."

Marci laughed. "I know, Carrie, but what can you do? That's the way things are sometimes."

"Well, I'm going to talk to her," Carrie said with determination.

"Good luck," Marci said. "It'll work out."

Carrie hung up the phone and went to bed. She scrunched her face into the pillow, but she couldn't sleep. Just when things were finally going right on the soccer team, Nicole had to get mad at her. Life was so unfair. She sighed as she drifted off to sleep.

On Saturday morning Carrie opened her eyes slowly and peered at the clock beside her bed. Seven-thirty. She tried to go back to sleep, but she was too excited about seeing Annie. She climbed out of bed, took a shower, read *Seventeen* all the way through, and drank a glass of juice. At nine o'clock she went over to Marci's. Marci was already sitting on her front porch.

"Hi," Marci said. "Nicole's on her way. And then I have a surprise for you."

"Annie?"

Marci smiled mysteriously. "You'll see," she said.

After a few minutes, Nicole joined them.

"Have you heard from Annie?" she asked, avoiding Carrie's eyes.

Marci nodded and smiled. "She called. She's on her way over."

The girls sat on the porch for five minutes without talking. It was probably a record of some sort. After what seemed like ages, Annie ran down the sidewalk toward them.

The girls jumped and hugged her.

"Where have you *been*?" Carrie cried.

"I've been away," Annie said. "And now I'm back."

Annie sat on the porch and looked at her friends. After a while a shy smile began to play at the corners of her lips, and before long she was smiling her special, magical, Annie smile. "*Boy*, am I glad to be back," she said.

Everyone agreed that it was wonderful to have her back.

"Where *were* you?" Nicole asked.

"Toledo."

"Toledo?" Marci said. "Toledo? What were you doing in Toledo?"

Annie laughed. "I almost ended up there for good. We went for a visit, because my Dad was going to start a new job there. We even told Mr. Freid."

Marci and Carrie glanced at each other. "You didn't tell *us*," Carrie said.

Annie blushed. "I'm really sorry, you guys. I couldn't. It was a big secret. Dad didn't want the people he works for now to know about it."

"Well, what happened?" Marci asked. "Why'd you come back?"

Annie pulled herself to her feet. "Because we like it here," she said. "Even my Dad decided that he likes it here. So we came back."

"Well, please don't go away again without telling us," Nicole said. "You scared us half to death."

"Sorry, I couldn't help it," Annie said. She hugged them again. "I'm so glad to see you all. Now, you have fifteen minutes to tell me everything that's happened since I left, and then I have to go and finish unpacking.''

Marci and Carrie laughed. Even Nicole managed a chuckle. ''I think we'll have to save it for later,'' Marci said.

''Oh,'' Annie said, ''that means a lot has happened since I've been gone.''

Fifteen minutes were definitely not long enough to tell Annie about Petie and Dave, and the soccer dilemma, and the plummeting computer stock.

''How about tonight?'' Annie said. ''Maybe we could get together?''

''I can't,'' Nicole said. ''The play's tonight.''

Carrie shot a meaningful glance at Marci.

Annie caught it and frowned. Then she shrugged and said, ''Oh, I forgot. We can get together after that.'' She looked so happy. ''I'm so glad I got back in time.''

The girls talked for a while, and when the fifteen minutes were up, Annie looked at her watch and jumped to her feet.

''Gotta go,'' she said.

Carrie stood up and walked to the corner with her.

''I've got a lot to talk to you about,'' Carrie said. ''I'll call you later.''

''Okay,'' Annie agreed. ''But what's up?''

''I'll tell you later, but this kid we've been baby-sitting for has a brother, and Nicole likes him, and . . . ''

"Uh, oh, let me guess. Does he like you?"

Carrie nodded. "And there's another thing," she said. "It's about the school play. Nicole doesn't want anyone to come, and she won't tell us why."

"I remember," Annie said. "I guess we'll have to wait until tonight."

"I don't know, Annie. Do you think we should go?"

"I think so. What kind of best friends wouldn't show up opening night?" Annie asked.

"But what about Nicole?"

"It'll be all right. Sometimes Nicole is too dramatic about things."

Carrie wasn't so sure. After all, Annie hadn't been around for a while. Annie might be right about the play, but she didn't understand how much Nicole seemed to care about Dave.

As Annie turned the corner, Carrie headed back to Marci's. Marci and Nicole were still sitting on the porch.

"Do we have to baby-sit Petie today?" she asked as she sat down next to Marci.

"Yeah," Marci replied. "Mrs. Franklin wants to go shopping this afternoon—*without Petie.*"

All of them smiled at that.

"Who's turn is it?" Carrie asked Marci.

"Mine," Nicole said.

"Again?" asked Carrie. "I thought it was my turn."

Marci stood up and went inside. In a few minutes

she was back. "According to my schedule," she said, "it's Annie's turn."

"I'll tell her," Nicole said quickly.

Carrie shrugged. "Okay. I have a lot to do anyway."

When Nicole got home, she called Annie.

"Marci already called," Annie said. "Guess I'll get to meet the infamous Petie today."

"Tell you what," Nicole suggested. "Why don't we both go? I need to get my mind off the play tonight, anyway. I'll pick you up at one."

At one o'clock Nicole rang Annie's doorbell, and they walked over to Petie's together.

Petie was sitting on the front porch when they arrived. He had his feet up on the railing and he was singing a strange song.

"What's that?" Nicole asked.

"It's called '248 Things That Start With T.' "

"And what number are you on now?" Annie groaned.

"Three," Petie said. "That's the one about the tiger." He peered at Annie. "I know who you are."

"You do?" Annie was a little surprised since she'd never met Petie.

"Sure." Petie looked pleased with himself. "You're Annie, the missing person."

Annie looked at Nicole, who said, "Who knows how he finds everything out? I think he has ESP."

Petie continued with his song.

Annie turned and shot Nicole a dismayed look. "Do we have to listen to a song about 248 things that start with T?" she asked.

Nicole shook her head and smiled. "Not if we're smart," she said. "Leave it to me."

"Hey, Petie," she said. "Bet you can't finish that song in an hour."

"Bet I can."

"Well, you stay right where you are and give it your all, okay?"

"Sure," Petie said. "And that way I'll be out of your way while you two are gossiping, right?"

Nicole and Annie burst out laughing. "That's right," Nicole said as they walked into the house, leaving Petie to finish his song.

Chapter 10

At six o'clock, Carrie's phone rang. "Hi," said a boy's voice. "It's Dave."

"Hi, Dave," Carrie said unenthusiastically.

"I'm calling about the play," Dave said. "I'm taking Petie. He seems to think Nicole needs him. What time does it start?"

Carrie was silent for a moment, and then she said, "You should get there at about a quarter to eight. It starts at eight."

"I guess I'll see you there," Dave said.

Carrie was beginning to get nervous. She didn't want to see Dave there, or at least she didn't want to see Nicole seeing Dave there with her.

"I'm going with my parents," Carrie lied, then quickly said good-bye and hung up the phone. She immediately dialed Annie's number.

"Dave called," Carrie said as soon as Annie said hello. "Did you meet him today?"

Annie said that she hadn't. "He wasn't around. What did he say?"

"He said he'd see me at the play."

"That sounds nice."

"I told him I was going with my parents."

"I didn't know your parents were going."

Carrie hesitated. "Well, they're not. I lied. I don't want to hurt Nicole's feelings anymore."

"I think everyone is acting a little silly about this," Annie said gently.

Carrie was feeling that, too. She'd try to resolve it with Nicole tonight.

When Annie, Marci, and Carrie got to the school auditorium that night, they were all excited. They quickly got their programs and settled into the first row. Carrie sat in the middle so that no one but Marci and Annie could sit beside her. She opened her program and looked for Nicole's name. It was listed second. Nicole Tucker—Mrs. Kirkland.

"Look," Carrie whispered. "She's second."

Someone tapped Carrie on the shoulder. Carrie turned around and faced Dave. "Hi," she said sheepishly.

"Aren't you going to introduce me to your parents?"

Carrie laughed nervously. "Annie and Marci," she said, "meet Dave."

"You two don't look much like parents to me," Dave said with a smile.

Carrie laughed again, which started Dave laughing, and before too long they were all doubled over in hysterics.

"Where's Petie?" Carrie asked when she could catch her breath.

"He went backstage," Dave said. "He said Nicole might need him." Suddenly the lights blinked, and the audience took their seats.

The curtain opened to show Mr. Kirkland, actually an actor made up to look like a middle-aged man, seated in a large easy chair in front of the fireplace. He was reading a book and listening to a record. After a moment, the record stuck, and Mr. Kirkland looked up from his book.

All of a sudden Nicole's voice boomed out from backstage.

"The record, darling," she called.

The girls heard a rustling sound, and then Nicole burst through a doorway in the back of the stage.

"I *don't* believe it," Annie gasped.

"She's *huge,*" Marci said.

Now they understood why Nicole hadn't wanted them to come to her play. She must have been embarrassed about her costume because she looked like she'd gained fifty pounds. She positively waddled when she walked.

As the play continued, however, it was clear that

Nicole was the real star. Toward the end of the first act, she moved toward center stage and began a monologue. She had said four sentences when she looked down and saw the rest of the Squad. She grinned bravely and continued speaking. Then she noticed Dave and stopped. She opened her mouth, but nothing came out. She looked away from Dave and tried to speak, but still nothing came out. Nicole looked as if she were about to faint.

Suddenly, a small voice came from the wings. " 'And I've been slaving in this house all my life.' "

The voice hit Nicole like a slap in the face. She repeated the line, and from then on the monologue went smoothly. When she finished, Dave leaned over and tapped Carrie on the shoulder. "I think we've found Petie," he said.

"That was Petie, all right," Marci said.

"Petie saves the day," Annie laughed.

Mr. Kirkland moved to center stage and started to speak. He said his first line. He said his second line. And he was about to say his next line when Petie said it for him.

The actor turned to the side and glared.

Marci poked Annie. "Oh, boy," she said. "Now we're in for it."

The audience could hear a bustling backstage and Petie's voice saying, "It's your turn. Get out there."

Suddenly a boy dressed as a grandfather was pushed onto the stage. The boy composed himself and said, "Sorry I'm late."

"No, no," Petie whispered much too loudly. "You're not sorry you're late. You're sorry you're early."

Suddenly someone raced down the aisle and ran up the stage steps.

"That's the director," Carrie told the others.

"What do you bet Petie will be joining us soon?" Dave whispered.

The words were hardly out of his mouth when Petie almost flew down the stage steps.

Dave got up to rescue him and brought him back to his seat.

When the play was over, Nicole waddled to the front of the stage and tried to bow. She was so large that she couldn't even lean over. So she curtsied. The audience cheered and whistled.

Carrie jumped up from her seat, and so did Annie, Marci, Dave, and Petie. Soon everyone was on their feet, clapping for the girl in the fat suit.

Carrie, Annie, and Marci ran up the back stairs and went backstage to wait for their friend. She came through the curtain, then returned for another bow. Carrie hugged her, and then she laughed.

"You're large," she said.

"You can say that again," Nicole laughed.

Carrie put her arm around Nicole. "It didn't matter," she said. "You were wonderful."

"You sure were," Annie and Marci said together.

"I'll agree with that," Dave said.

Nicole turned and smiled at him. "Thanks, Dave," she said. "It was nice of you to come."

"I wouldn't have missed it," he said, "and neither would Petie."

The girls looked at each other.

"Petie," they said together. And then they groaned. "He saved my life," Nicole said. "He just got carried away. That's all."

"I'm a hero. I'm a star," Petie yelled. "I'm every great person you've ever heard of rolled into one. You should be proud to know me."

Dave grabbed him under the arms and picked him up. He raised him higher and higher until his feet were way off the ground. Petie was kicking furiously.

"All right, star," Marci said, "how about if we throw you a party in my basement? It starts in half an hour."

Chapter 11

The Super Squad led Petie and Dave back to Marci's house. On the way they stopped to buy soda and pizzas. When they were settled in the basement, Marci called the gathering to order. She pulled a piece of pizza out of the box and raised it in the air.

"Ladies and gentlemen," she began, "this party is in honor of our actress and friend Nicole and her brilliant coach Petie. I'm sure that everyone agrees that they both did a super job."

Everyone applauded and raised their slices of pizza.

"I think Petie should be made an honorary member of the Squad," Marci went on. "Everyone who agrees, say 'Aye.' "

"Aye," shouted Carrie and Nicole and Annie.

"How about me?" Dave said. "Don't I get to be an honorary member, too?"

Everyone laughed.

"What do you think, Carrie?" Nicole said.

"It's up to you," Carrie said.

Nicole and Carrie looked at each other and smiled.

"Friends?" Carrie asked.

"Friends," Nicole agreed.

Annie leaned closer to Marci and tapped her on the shoulder.

"What's going on?" she whispered.

"Judging from past experience," Marci said, "I'd say Nicole's in love."

"With Dave?"

Marci laughed. "From the looks of it, I'd say no. Probably someone she met backstage."

Nicole and Carrie walked over to Dave. Nicole linked her arm with his left arm. Carrie linked her arm with his right.

"Welcome, honorary member," they said together.

"Now let's play some Ping-Pong," Carrie added.

"Great," Dave said. "I'll be your partner."

Carrie shook her head vigorously. "No way," she said. "I'm going to be Nicole's partner. You have to choose someone else."

"How about me?" Petie said. "I'm the star of the evening."

Dave laughed and tossed a paddle to Petie. "You're on," he said. "Let's beat these two."

Of course, they didn't have a chance. Nicole and Carrie won all three games, and then Annie and Marci beat the boys in three straight.

"This is no fun," Petie said after the sixth game.

They sat down to catch their breath, and Marci put some music on. "You know, Petie," she said, "this baby-sitting job is over as of today. I heard Monday you start computer class, so you won't be needing a baby sitter."

"I want some money," Nicole announced.

Everyone looked at Marci.

"Can't," Marci said. "Impossible. Out of the question. All the money's tied up in a computer stock that's bound to make us millionaires."

"What stock is that?" Carrie asked. "Is it the same one?"

Marci admitted that it was.

"How's it doing?" Carrie asked.

"Better."

"How much better?"

"Well," Marci said slowly, "it's doing better than yesterday—well, a little better, at least."

Carrie stood up and put on her jacket. "I can see that we're not going to get paid again."

Everyone else stood up and followed Carrie up the stairs.

"Will you be here for our next new assignment?" Marci called after them. "I've got something great lined up."

Everyone groaned. "Don't tell us now. Give us the good news later."

"But I'm not buying a new tennis racket yet," Carrie said.

"It's a good thing we're all such good friends," Nicole said with a grin, "because no one in their right mind would be working for no money at all."

Marci waved good-bye, then went down to the basement and sat in front of the computer terminal.

"Somehow," she said to herself, "if I just work a little harder, we'll all be millionaires before we know it."